For Ruby.
A.H. Benjamin

To my mama and papa who always interpreted
my growling in such a nice way.
Merel Eyckerman

What's That Terrible Growl?
Somos8 Series

© Text: A.H. Benjamin, 2018
© Illustrations: Merel Eyckerman, 2018
© Edition: NubeOcho, 2019
www.nubeocho.com · hello@nubeocho.com

Text editing: Eva Burke and Rebecca Packard

First edition: 2019
ISBN: 978-84-17123-55-0

Printed in China by Asia Pacific Offset,
respecting international labor standards.

WHaT'S THaT TERRIBLE GROWL?

A.H. BENJAMIN
MEREL EYCKERMAN

nubeOCHO

What's that terrible

GROWL?

Is it a **big, hairy bear** from the dark woods?

What does **it want?**

GGRRR

G G R R R R R R R R R R R R R R R r r

What's that terrible GROWL?

Is it a hungry, ferocious lion from the savannah?

What does it want?

What's that terrible

GROWL?

Is it an angry, stumpy gorilla
from the misty mountains?

What does it want?

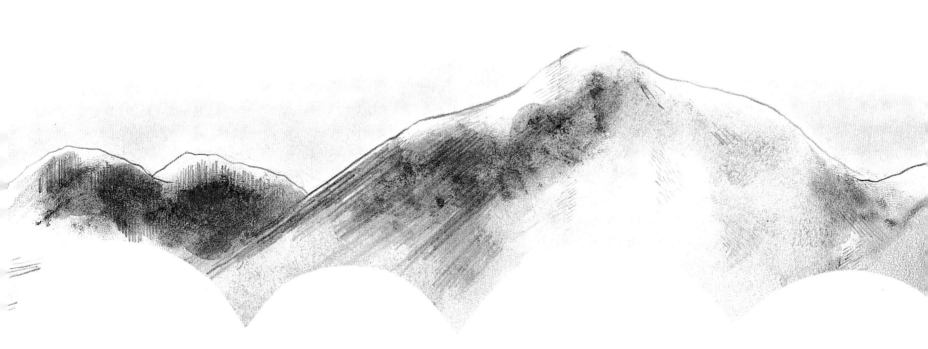

What's that terrible

GROWL?

Is it a **mean, ugly ogre**
who lives in a castle of bones?

What does **it want?**

What's that terrible

GROWL?

Is it a **scaly, fire-breathing dragon** from a far-off land?

What does **it want?**

What's that **terrible**

GROWL?

Is it a **giant, slimy worm**
from deep underground?

What does **it want?**

GGGRRRRR

GGRRRRRR

What's that **terrible**

GROWL?

Is it a **spiky, green sea monster**
from the bottom of the ocean?

What does **it want?**

What's that **terrible**

GROWL?

Is it a **ten-eyed, spotty creature** from outer space?

What does **it want?**

GRRRRRR

What's that **terrible**

GROWL?

Who's making it?

Is it...

...a **bear**... a **lion**...
a **gorilla**... an **ogre**...
a **dragon**... a giant **worm**...
a **sea monster**...

Or a **creature** from outer space?

No!

It's only…

RUBY!

"Sorry, sweetie," said Mum. "We didn't realize you wanted **Grrrrrr…** Here it is!"

Ruby smiled happily
and continued playing
with her **brother**
and her **dinosaur…**
Grrrrrr!

7